Slingstones

Slingstones

Mmhonlumo Kikon

Published by
Rupa Publications India Pvt. Ltd 2021
7/16, Ansari Road, Daryaganj
New Delhi 110002

Sales centres:
Allahabad Bengaluru Chennai
Hyderabad Jaipur Kathmandu
Kolkata Mumbai

Copyright © Mmhonlumo Kikon 2021

This is a work of fiction. Names, characters, places and incidents are either the product of the author's imagination or are used fictitiously and any resemblance to any actual person, living or dead, events or locales is entirely coincidental.

All rights reserved.

No part of this publication may be reproduced, transmitted, or stored in a retrieval system, in any form or by any means, electronic, mechanical, photocopying, recording or otherwise, without the prior permission of the publisher.

ISBN: 978-93-90547-38-8

Second impression 2021

10 9 8 7 6 5 4 3 2

Printed at Gopsons Papers Ltd.

This book is sold subject to the condition that it shall not, by way of trade or otherwise, be lent, resold, hired out, or otherwise circulated, without the publisher's prior consent, in any form of binding or cover other than that in which it is published.

*To Zanbow and Tsenyimo,
my grandfather and father,
both now deceased.*

Contents

Stars	1
Lead Them Unto Death	2
Missionaries	3
Labour for Britain	5
Grandma's Curse	6
Ripe Forest	8
Portrait of a Leader	9
Original Offspring	10
The Spirit of Memory	12
A Disturbing Dream	14
Siberian Quest for a Roosting Place	15
Deceptive Smile	17
Occupation	19
Engagement	21
The Thatch Mansion	22
Sesame Seed	24
Rare People	26
The Ambassador Car	27
The Bear Cub	29

The Chosen One	31
The House Guard	34
The Kitchen Garden	35
Twist	36
By the Warmth of a Fireplace	37
To Culture	38
Runaway Slaves of The Great Wall	39
Self-Worth	40
The Seed Sermon	42
The Japanese Gene	44
You are Crime	45
Apes of the East	47
Your Home is My Space	49
Immortal	51
Revelation's Wall	52
Give Us Your Worst	53
A Paid Version	55
A Calling	57
Afire	58
Bullet and Banana	59
Fortress	60
Swift By The Sword	62

Old Ones Freeze	64
Privilege of Suicide	65
Listless Fear	66
Sold Here: Farm Food	67
The Middleman	68
Grudge	69
Ethnographer	70
Off to Church	72
Half Plan	73
A Refuge of Old	74
In Doubt	76
Sweat for Opium	77
The Burden of Will	78
Hanging Bridge	79
Our Moon God	80
Soldiers of Fortune	81
To Wine and Dine	82
When Winter flew	84
When a Priest Invites You to Dinner	86
The Rain Prayer	87
An Unnatural Outbreak	89
Inside All of It	91

Private	93
Common Burden	96
Assurance	98
Queen	99
In Waiting	101
The Anointed	103
Songs	105
Sleep and Prayer	106
Acknowledgements	109

Stars

Grinding and halting,
erratic pitter-patter of the rain.
Submission of penance overdue,
they peek into the mirror's gaze.

Shift from the petty fixations,
of a minor in deep trouble—
over hunger, thirst, addiction,
exhibitionist tendencies, talents unborn—

Seeing a star,
in lieu of a reality show,
a real vain affair.

Lead Them Unto Death

Stir a generation,
Tear a path,
hustle towards the well-trodden rush,
Galvanize the normal,
forge the secure and the familiar,
Offer comfort to the lie,
Till the blue mountains,
A hoe in callused hands,
Before the river floods the plains.

Stir the rebels,
The dangerous minions,
The fake underlings,
The pruned bone.

Raise an army of imbeciles,
And lead them to wilderness.
Persist in limbo,
Till plague kills them all.

Missionaries

I thought,
woven craft,
bamboo or cane material
for loftier tapestry,
basketry is ancient art.

I saw,
a basket made to carry bamboo,
holding spring water,
and firewood,
head-strap over steady skulls.

I heard,
a pristine state ensconced,
indigenous, protected.

Then I saw,
those same heads carrying,
affixed to the same head-straps and baskets,

an American man and woman,
borne over the strong back and the stiff shoulder.

Labour for Britain

A hardy farmer
on a sunny day.
beads of sweat making
a bountiful harvest.

Merrymaking is fermenting rice,
inebriated men disrobing loin cloth,
dense tendons loosening,
Having run from conscription.

A warrior with a hundred heads,
glorified barbarian, decorated gladiator.
No man dare say his name wrong
was the first to explode, his nerves seething,
in all expeditions: virile.

Now, with shadowy ropes,
contained.
Now, a labour for Britain.

Grandma's Curse

Your mistress, Edwina,
smoking a pipe so vain,
unnoticed, reminiscing, you puffed,
skirts flew in easter winds,
you sang as the church bells rang.

Nehru, grandma's pet,
a wild boar, untamed in secret,
rice, rice and rice
was all we ate.

Grandma saw your Dakotas,
jhum fields now disturbed your flirtation,
it ruffled your peace.

For gay romance you would bomb.

Her nipples dry and breast taut,
cry baby suckled a milk-drop a day.

She cursed Nehru,
looking above the dark heavens,
'wait till you meet your enemies!'

Mao came to her in dreams,
a thousand miles to march now,
fingers pointing out the miles.
The PLA would march deep into the valley.

Ripe Forest

Herbs, fruits, wild apples,
gooseberries, and sometimes, red ants.
Nourished,
her breast replenished;

What some jacket-jackass never saw,
she savored in private,
in the thick of the forests,
wildflowers and animals,
but food,
but soothsayers of the world,
unnerving spirits,
but in the din of pride, a warm home.

Portrait of a Leader

Bell's palsy,
a trapped face,
inhibits winking at
your dog or cousin,
a bland response to humour.
Severity in paralysis;
not a handsome face, yet fame,
leadership, force of personality,
wealth, and a photograph in a golden frame,
makes the visage remarkable to behold.

Legend, rabble-rouser,
but a good theme,
for a cause.

He persists in the rustic sanity,
in the urban mad,
in the crazy, blood-baying, head-hunting,
gory glory chorus of a proud people.

Original Offspring

A famous village by raucous river,
feared and remote,
couched in the palm of a mountain.
whispers of a war, waged and lost,
with a superior foe,
unequal and unmatched
to the glory of having fought,
A lost war, a certainty—
yet they fought
in the unfettered hope.

Remember tales
of battles won by guile;
the war lost the same year
they saw short and scrawny soldiers
marching up the hill,
heaving and puffing as they met a fortress,
Daunting and unyielding.

Weapons were longer,
taller—if measured—
but spears rained on them, hurled on them
at the speed of a steep.
Gigantic boulders rolled,
hurting and smashing,
as it tumbled rapidly downhill,
acceleration and annihilation.

The Spirit of Memory

In Rangoon,
a tyre burst, a car stopped,
a meeting missed, and a mistress waited.

In Rangoon,
in an Orwellian tea shop,
a secret hideout, an open gaze,
a conspiracy to hatch, over a cup of tea.

Only punctures—
bald tyres needing replacement,
And yet, enough cars
for the white man,
repairing with cash.

The image puncturing and weaving,
enemies at the gates,
of desolate man in cotton vests,
as some resisted and sought.

Kinsmen fought, battles wreak,
Bitter-sweet, the heartburn of loss.

A victory sought—
one must rise,
as one must plot.
But one must will
an endless stream
tomorrow.

A Disturbing Dream

Chubby cheeks, cascading down the chin
as skin could no longer hold the face,
in a strange deformation,
a contortion so extreme—
like dough made in the dark of night,
kept for ages with the husks to dry.

Insane dream, of people dead and gone,
of triple murders committed
and the murderer seen, in heaven,
strolling the jade garden with Saint Paul,
discussing the meaning of faith.

In Christ's name we killed
for the promise of free ration,
and sought
an incestuous power
with our beloved tormentors.

Siberian Quest for a Roosting Place

Sometimes, the river beckons
wild feed of earth.
A tired beetle,
ants in a beeline for winter sun,
termites seeking rent
in Siberia;
food not scarce nor weather harsh,
undefinable tendencies,
in migration but a subtle habit.

Doyang, the green river in distress,
as regular guests
soar circles—
again and again and again,
in simulation but the form of a memory,
of different locations
strange responses,
lilting whisper of the wings,
in thousands, swishing and diving,
here rests their unusual abode.

Manna from heaven,
A reservoir of food despoiled,
swarming the fisherman,
pensive hands to shield truant eyes
Looking for meat,
And casting net for food deep inside
the green river.

Deceptive Smile

Blank faces carrying simple smiles,
no pretence as perfect as in mimicry,
nor a gentle heart falters,
hither-thither, pricks all follow.

You should see her questions,
suggestions as conversations,
query in songs,
declarations in praises,
appealing as the ever soft,
accepting, willing, purple ice.

Not so simple as it may seem,
or as pretentious it may sound;
melodious jingle of a form,
feeding words, stealing commands,
imposing kindness unforeseen, unbeknownst,
to the killjoy of a man who,
In happenstance, lived the life of a hermit,

The reading, bookish, rival lover who,
lacked the gut-wrenching of love.

A dirty crow,
scavenging on crumbs of kindness,
thrown in flirtatious tones,
scattered across bony streets,
lonely as a hunter,
hunting the haunted,
wounding the servile,
and performing a nun's innocence,
in a monastery full of rapists.

Occupation

I saw a doorman, glaring from afar
as I walked
past the illicit cars
to reach the revolving door.
And without smiling, a sunken dry face, pale eyes
devoid of remorse. I thought,
a wild gesture of the hands,
managed to scare me
into stern attention.

My eyes stared back at him,
then askance, sometimes at the slew of drivers
smoking and puffing in turns,
some weed, or so it seemed.
I stood, unfazed
as he put the scanner to my forehead.

I smiled, thinking he would return it,
as a comrade of thick lips,

'chinky' eyes, natural smile,
he would know my category,
my abysmal case,
as he asked me to offer identification.

As I left, I saw him, staring at me,
hiding my bright expensive phone,
I walked faster, rushed by the discomfort of his gaze.

I dreamt of him that night,
shouting at me
anger for something—I don't remember—
and, I was wearing a blue uniform,
the same cloth he wore at the door.

I swore,
I would visit him again.

Engagement

Sodden footpath,
mired in sedition.
A summer, all muddy and gay.

She walks to her fiancée's home,
to break the uneventful,
news of her engagement
to another man.

The Thatch Mansion

A bullet pierces through your mother tongue,
as the butt of the rifle imposes a decree on your motion;
Half in love, you seal a pact
and run,
away to the safest shore.

As soon as you know it is yours,
you pick up the rifle,
pluck a flower along the path,
and send it back to the armoury—
your mother mattered most to you.

Such crab you were fed in the ramshackle school
'I' became 'we' as you crossed the threshold,
certified by violence.
When no tools were found,
they inflicted the drill on the village.

Come, come now, to the thatch mansion,
of the sun-soaked wild gardens,
of bamboo groves and snake graves,
pig sties oozing prospective roasts,
fermented soybeans to toast;
you come and play me in my reedy bird's nest.

Sesame Seed

Sesame seed,
retrieved from the cache for a sombre occasion,
crushed in a wooden pot,
with a hand-held wooden pestle
regulating force with steady pressure;
as the water boils over the firewood,
and the sooty aluminium pot
receives the pulverized black seeds,
it dissolves,
like salt into the simmering pork;
red and soft with chilli powder
wiry pieces of dried bamboo-shoot dancing
with bubbles of hot water.
The fire burning as more logs are shoved,
and flame rises up,
and the smoke dissipates.

A relish, a taste, a delicacy, a recipe,
all forged on fire, sprinkled with sesame seeds.

Rare People

In rare seasons, rare as my uncle's grin,
some Jackals emerge to meet you,
relevant now for a reason,
as insignificant lost years found,
out to conduct a friendly trial.

Pithy comments, as if handed down
from heavenly abode,
as angelic voices,
bestow us with a favour.

And when the voice came,
it spoke of rain and sun,
as if it were born
all from the same mother.

The Ambassador Car

My mother scrubbed my caked face clean
with a wet cotton hand towel,
then, with her coarse harsh hands,
she wiped my face again,
squeezing my nose, dry of mucus.
And as I am, squirming in shame and self-pity,
goblet of tears collected as they roll down,
as the White Ambassador car approached,
stately and Imposing,
and eyes peered out of the windows,
my mother rubbed my sudden tears dry again.

She rushed to greet my friend, well combed
and neatly dressed, like a picture on my school
yearbook,
Why? she said, you are very kind.

She rubbed me again in front of him,
And showed him the rusted tin roof,

scraggly and decaying,
when I had already showed him
another place for the pick-up.

Why waste clean clothes to play in the mud,
in the sand, with leftover paints,
experimenting with colours and dirt.

The Bear Cub

A cub lay in a barn,
and the mother bear down the ravine,
flies buzzing over her coagulated furs;
the lumbering giant's body was slowly decomposing.
For over a week, none of the hunters
could figure out a way out, down
the steep and rugged ravine
with no path in sight,
and such as only mountain goats could find.

Soon, the sighted leopard will find a way
where the hunters dare not try.

As the cub was lifted
moments after her eyes saw
her mother toss off the cliff—
the shot surely tilting her balance.

And now, the cub lay in a barn,
the chain long enough
for her to move around the iron rod.

The Chosen One

On a spur, in a freakish moment
improvising information,
and delivering it with finesse,
like it were an original composition,
an ultimate signature
between shivering lips and fluttering beard.

Speaking with unassuming authority,
he fabricated a sound verdict.

Between dusk and dawn,
managing a snoring rest and a sleep,
surprising even the cock
the riser of an early morning.

He conjured another concoction
in his laboratory,
calling it 'The Liar's Incubation Hub'.

And there, with amazing speed,
a fictitious truth after another,
a creative feat,
a pursuit to embarrass Machiavelli,
and living up to the fame,
his fluency was spontaneity.

He was in his element
when a durbar was held
He revelled in eyes
fixated on his torso.

He held forth
on subversive schemes,
And how he beguiled
so many emissaries from the Palace.

Years of slog, flogging,
betrayals, cheating, greasing palms and carrying loads,

nights of perfecting lies,
selling his allies,
conjuring a devious system,
to becoming the beloved of the righteous,
a method so clinical,
even his detractors worshipped this studied pose.

The House Guard

From the rat hole, you witness a visage of nerves,
a head, sliding up in slow motion,
in trepidation, eyeballs encircling the surroundings
looking, looking for a sniper,
or a predator,
ready to bite if a spider nears,
a fizzle here, shrill and angry.

Yes, it is my turf,
my house to protect and care for,
to harass and intimidate,
and all who approach,
if even as much as their shadow lingers
at the border.

I shall rain on them napalm;
I shall spit venom and spew poison with my tongue.

The Kitchen Garden

Surveying all the affairs of the garden,
overgrown fussy weeds
consuming the gardener's time,

Spying upon an aversion
a beast of a worm;
Is it political or not?

Consider the angst of the unmentioned farm sickle
when sweet cucumber is on the rise,
alongside the Naga King chilly

like meeting constraints
struggling for an excuse
To make nature appear spoiled.

Ants loiter
up the ladies finger,
and the yellow tomatoes and ginger leaves.

Snip-snap, swish, flash, out you all go to burn.

Twist

Twist the rubbery tongue at once—
a sudden use of flippant terms,
an inversion of infrequent commitments,
relying deep on semantics—only to confuse.

When you seek to perfect twisting,
as if your uncouth tongue needs the practice,
and you miss the liminal space of habit.

Your name is anyways difficult to pronounce,
and your face suspicious.
I am sure, my story is not your history.

Even as we plea the same country,
in search of common diversity,
to relearn each other as we rename,
to live together as one intolerable,
we seek to dominate within one's mind,
and square it with indomitable spirit.

By the Warmth of a Fireplace

A kitchen
is a burning fireplace,
logs of wood and fire;
a crackling fire
and a warm bedside.

As knuckles cracked,
in a blanket,
upon the chiselled cot;
smoke engulfs you,
nostrils light up to the particles
of unseen ash.

You become incense,
fire smoke, pork broth boiling,
luscious bamboo shoot;
steaming trails of aroma.
Fire is food,
Life is pork
and bamboo-shoot.

To Culture

It was you.
A pretence of culture;
you made appearances
tall like sunflower stalk.

A worn body,
a torn soul,
a skin shed,
the green snake in a coiled mood,
to acquire anew,
and strip away the old.

From Underneath the decay,
worn clothes torn asunder—
and for how many aeons
did you survive?
Pray tell me, how many avatars you assumed
to become you?
And knowing,
not knowing, culture was you.

Runaway Slaves of The Great Wall

You runaway slave,
burden of forced labour,
Yes, you; lazy,
rebellious, unambiguous, animists.
How disinterested you are,
in walls and ambitions,
lacking skills to carry stone,
to help build a fortress,
and to be part of
Unremembered history.

Chipping stones is craft;
You see and learn,
No, not the skills of engineering,
or that of good genes.
Just your dirty hands
to touch the hammer,
enough to at least handle a tool.

Self-Worth

So, you deny
the me-in-you,
Soul-friend and spirit-enemy,
your being and existence
enmeshed through my bones;
We die
to seek eternity.

Your waste, your ego,
your tangling hair:
all become you.

We wish to coexist,
cohabit, copulate.
In silvery tongues eschew,
rubbing silken-soft embraces,
with your denial, your betrayal.

So your colours are new,
signifying you,
consuming all of you,
long ago, when the demons chewed,
like pulp between teeth for pleasure.

Your past is me,
Your present is new,
You deny inheritance,
You despoil the soul, you piss on the spirit,
for the same purpose,

Your present is hell.

The Seed Sermon

A sermon was delivered,
as prophetic as the croaking of toads—
Alighting from an old jeep,
left from world wars,
within a pine forests,
leaving trails of marauding Japanese—
by a short man,
brimming with ambitions.

A voice so smooth,
few would lean away,
holding back a yawn,
shoulder on a birch tree too;
a seedy brilliance
for birds and insects to cheer.

Embalm, preserve your tribal instincts,
Outstrip all newness,
Power a nation,

Ignore a thought,
a silly notion.
He said, you would Mould,
Reshape,
Realign,
If the American Mission was white,
Ours is red.

The Japanese Gene

Leave the rice beer to dry,
hang it tall in a bamboo pole,
Bloodthirsty samurai of distant regions,
white man's religions
dampening your soil;
born a Naga,
with Japanese seed.

Sounds, like dust,
convey history in buckets;
bury your head in peace;
As unto dust,
you shall rise.

Like the headgear,
ungainly worn.

You are Crime

You lure, bring yourself,
against the burning tide,
the million hopes,
the small sobs,
for distracted souls, they fly,
falling from the skies,
scorn fiercely,
and then, love meekly.

Seasons in turmoil,
seasons merciful,
shoes of leather in dessert foil,
a storm of farce
blowing upon your face.
Eat your shrine
as you worship pride.

You are crime
Black as coal

greed so ossified,
you are in love,
insignificant as dirt.

Apes of the East

Rejoice in the pain of death,
cry inside the wave of glory you expect,
for you will be assaulted—not once,
for being you,
and your people are there in you.
The violence heaped on you,
is also the love heaped on you.

But you know that already.

They made a page of you,
monkeys, jumping, leaping across,
you, semblance of a human—
of which species?
of which race
or deracinated synonyms,
or stereotypical slurs?
Yes,
they made you,
when you were out playing soccer.

At the Lodhi Gardens,
they were visited by wild beasts
from a wild world.

Your Home is My Space

For Gramsci spotted you in the prison, where he jotted words
in his notebooks, just then,
saw they had made a space,
an otherness, but not you.
They saw you—unravished, untouched—but
they built their cities
on your oil, your tea gardens.
They even called it a revenue,
a stream where black gold abounds,
as milk must flow black,
they build their cities.

Prison was greasy,
excruciating.
Even couched in the deafening silence of the jungle,
Beside birds and insects,
vying now for their stolen lands
taken by the prophet of gloom,

carrying the burden of his ancestors,
who lost a generation.

A tomb for amnesia,
And so, the stirred souls gathered,
Swore to bow but only in discord,

Hallelujah! To the traitors!

Immortal

Lift a stone
atop a broken wall;
see if it stands
the test of time.
As sure as your arms lift,
so swift shall be the fall.

Lift again, with the strength of Samson,
the slaves of yore,
of the philistines in Egypt,
A life may emerge
in the hearts of men,
in a shame distilled.

Revelation's Wall

You broke the wall of misery
in a single day,
in one fell swoop,
of your imagined self—
as removed from the past
as it was,
it still withstood time.

Anarchy and peace
hand in hand,
in unison went,
as you preached the unthinkable.
Of pork and beef
of taxes unknown
of tropes unthought,
in our jungle
atop the hills,
across the mountains,
beyond the skies.

Give Us Your Worst

Your worst is best for us.
We are pleased to admit it
into our hall of fame,
make exquisite frames to house them.
When we are done,
we will fix them there—on our walls,
within our hallowed meeting halls—
next to our equally great leader.

Give us the illiterate,
even the literate who no longer read
as long as a patriot they be,
and their heart loves the nation.
Knowledge is the smallest concern,
only cooperation brushing aside any discomfort.

Thus a nation is build,
with discipline and obedience,
where leaders and followers live together.

A Paid Version

If he were to beg,
In a wanton fit, in savvy gestures,
holding out an empty brown sack?
Is it a desire, a choice, or a condition?
Hapless, a tightrope, the wizardry
of people clinging on.

Unpivoted stars behold,
in Patkai hills,
over the Saramati Mountains,
where, on the Chindwin river,
shimmers the silver moon; there,
he saw a vision.

A verdant song and even birds glide
as the song swells,
into a frivolous tune,

churning a melody, an idea
a war cry,
echoing a call,
a piper's voice.

A Calling

Surely the wind,
so harsh, severe, chilly,
must fell as it sways,
and when it is not whooshing, swirling
an uprooted and unruly teak,
then wild elephants are pulled astray.

There, he whistled, whispered in turns,
a Mission.

No less than the call of the wild,
plucked,
pricked from the inane routine,
awakened from sun-dried husks
into a flutter of gold rush.

Afire

Seek no peace yet,
with the treacherous past.

Never desire either,
at such measured levels.

Watch the water flow,
run down its normal course.

Toil for none,
be simple, servile and lie prostrate.

In life or death,
or when hallowed ancestors
light a fire,
the warmth and glow transforming nature—

Sometimes, witches burnt here,
Sickle and broom aflame.

Bullet and Banana

This fire, this crackling sound,
moving with haste,

A thought came, such a wild idea,
a banana stem, its juicy stalk,
so thick and round,
could douse that fire,
piercing right through.

With this idea wrestled,
a deadly foe, a deadlier fire,
a bullet,
an explosive hitherto unknown.

Out the muzzle-loading gun,
rang the shot of power,
of domination,
and a story rewritten.

Fortress

Alder tree, warped,
Crooked warts, eye of a bird—adorning.
Evenly cut, erected upright,
into a wooden post.
A village's defence,
an ugly stockade.

Approaching enemies,
Who not being near,
Still gathered heads,
Or rather, bodies, still alive,
still quivering,
fallen, one after the other,
and in horror, the village saw,
their supine warriors surrender.

It seemed like a campaign,
a battle, a skirmish,

for the sick,
neither strong, nor surrendering, nor responding,

Conceit mangling humiliation,
as they lay down their lives,
and held their arms with pride.

At the end, atop the granary,
once storing only grains of life,
flew high,
a new symbol,
called a flag.

Swift By The Sword

On the same dreary day,
that swift arrows flew,
matching the swords of time,
both the father and son,
were killed on the battlefield.

Led by desire
and an unquenchable thirst,
in perpetual debt to the vengeful heart;
panting in despair,
wanting to maim and kill.
In turn, both felled by that unsuspecting desire.

A thousand times more sinister,
the chalet carried poison
of an unwanted time,
of the unsought manifesto,

in the hourly destiny,
set by the divine.

Surely, we must have sought its blessing.

Old Ones Freeze

In the killing fields, do you remember
the temples wrought with
the sweat and tears of the warriors?
the blood spilled with sanction
the unborn and the wounded?

Swords smeared with filth,
spewing and moulting over dismembered heads,
as muscles and sinews roared
to roast the enemies in thought,
much before the act.

A broken saint
whose only counsel
we must disobey,
to survive the wrath of desire.

We must embrace the lust of the flesh,
the warmth,
wrapping over the biting cold.

Privilege of Suicide

There is no end
to the stillborn;
Celebrated in grief as it is
wrapped in muslin (imagine),
readied for a farewell.

The vapour of breath,
afloat in the air only a scent, the essence,

So it was to him that dreamt a war so unwanted—

Wounded, yet he ran,
into a cave where no weapons
could pierce his heart.
And having found shelter,
he did
what his enemies ought to do—
he ended his only life.

Listless Fear

Is dying the death of us?
Do you whisper softly,
amidst growing shrieks?

A ventilator-sentence for life;
A Siamese twin on you,
Fears blow by as we see, we feel,
panic-ridden.
Or is it the long listless wait?

Is fear your only companion, lasting
confusion in panic so normal?
In random, in fate,
resurfacing.
Is it now a disease?

Sane voices assure,
as all seem wayward,
unknown and rattled, the more we know,
the more we fear.

Sold Here: Farm Food

Red chillies, scattered hither-tither in the fields.
Sprouts, organic, fresh as desire,
Green cabbages, rolling with laughter,
while unseen quantities,
in street corners abound,
carted by restless farmers,
burning with thirst.

Rows and rows of cheap plenty,
left on the roadside dirt veg,
an open, free, wide market,
as present as the trees, as ignored as the air.

Surplus,
No 'pesticide-free' board drafted;
the Land of plenty,
the Land of no farce.

The Middleman

In verdant fields, rice is grown
In a season, it was sown.
All the corn we ate
growing tall by the side.

Even before the harvest,
surreptitious and silent,
a beaver has stolen a deal.

Soft paws, softer moves,
to compete—a sickening old profession;
that was before, that you would say.

Carelessly, observing,
wheels of fortune turn.
Is it greased always, as price is set
on delivery?

Grudge

In the end
your mind wanders as if lost
on purpose,
over a case
as mundane
as a grudge.

In disagreement,
ever since your loss
induced dark deeds,
with no shame to mention,
to the angel of seduction,
And the jealous, hideous apprentice,
who exposed you to her!

Ethnographer

He stood to sing a war cry
having been slapped in the face—
a petty thing,
and such a waste of honour.

Silly warrior, dwelling in scorn.

What strange names to have?
Warrior, head-hunter,
farmer, feast-giver;
merits a joke.

In pissing games, he wins.

He hunts heads in battle,
He tends the fields.
Does he even know,
he is but the mane
of a dead lion?

He considered his skin red,
He thought the British did too;
Colour-blind, maybe?
Awe-inspiring description.

Laughable man,
and as easily hurt
as easily as he considered the ethnographer a friend.

Off to Church

Grandma went to the church
in search of healing.
That's where they said she would find it;
just sit in the front,
near the pulpit.

She sat in the front, as told,
must listen closely, as she was
hard of hearing,
as age was catching up,

'Anytime' they said, 'she might die.'

When grandma returned home,
she told her neighbour,
to bring the wild boar meat,
dried by the fireplace.

She said she needs it for dinner.

Half Plan

Ever felt like
getting parts of you
unshackled over a plan,
unsure still,
uncorking wisdom,
wizening up before you are ready,
chest thumbing, heartbeats going awry—

Sounds like an internship,
overcoming-the-fear baby step,
before calm sweeps in again.

Running to build castles,
imagine the insanity,
When, as prey, you tell your priests,
I will eat your madness, and soon.

Damnation.

A Refuge of Old

Whoever, you say,
left behind a camera,
stuffed inside a tiny yellow teddy bear,
sitting like an unseen customer,
atop a mandatory mahogany table,
hovering around, like a sad bee.

A sobering escape,
from the neighbourhood,
a refuge of old, straddled between histories.
Everyone knew it was coming,
to take him home
to take him to his escape.

He lied to his pet,
a brown lazy cat,
about his uncertain destination.

Squeezing out a cure from
the poison hemlock he drank,
to be sure of its efficacy,
and all the while, strangers sleep on unmitigated urges.

In Doubt

It was always the refuge,
you assumed,
And probably, you may be right.
Since in doubt,
you seek—

—a horror much lesser,
almost risky,
ephemeral,
given the trust.

So, when appearances stink,
sue a hefty fee.

Sweat for Opium

The humid air tears through the summer;
a weary traveller must know,
thrown in the throes,
of a pandemic scare,
birthing a thousand new ways
to shift opium,
to worship things,
to profit the lawless.

Your silver bullet dripping through the dreary
plantations,
with thick saliva,
unhinging a regime;
the ailing land,
of a vigour most vicious.

The Burden of Will

Where goes the cry so shrill?
Now in the absence of any frills,
in night or day of restrictions;
In whose arms shall we rest
the burden of our collective will?

A society of timid people,
said Hannah Arendt,
Ah, but a society of harmful people,
said the savage.

Insipid, dull and edgy,
picking on anything in sight
to soothe the fickle minds
roaming the labyrinths of falsehood.

Hanging Bridge

In my moods reminiscent
of the dark days,
carried over by tradition,
like the plume
of a hornbill,
transfixed for ages;
I ponder,
why did we leave
the years so spread,
avoiding alligators,
leaning left and right,
balancing with nature's cordage,
hugging tightly the sturdy Oak?

Our Moon God

We are animists,
trapped hunters of the soul,
and that's where the outrage begins.

Neil Armstrong landed on the moon, but
it was our god
he desecrated with his small leap.

How could he even dare
to step on our deity,
and Trample on our worship?

Perhaps, they sent in the missionaries
to our land,
so our minds could grow accustomed,
to a new ritual,
a servility of cantankerous vacuum,
as they trampled on our gods.

Soldiers of Fortune

Shorter than a tall dwarf,
a pair of stocky calves, a sturdy mien,
rounded and gloomy;
which village produces such men?

A soldier of fortune,
conscripted with promises from Canaan,
rifle-armed to counter sharpened daos,
and frilled with poison-dipped spears;
from western Myanmar Hills,
what chaos did they leave behind
to dwell on such misery?

To *Wine* and Dine

This did the cacophonic inheritance converge
in seedy tongues of those slimy foes,
who exposed and admitted?

Lies told and retold
in the kitchen,
by the fireplace,
while embers slowly flickered to ashes,
and the smoke billowed across the neighbourhood
to the villages and to the towns,
as sunlight and rain engulfed the inhabitants.

It was the season of wild apples,
wine to make a mad rush
to pick the best, the potent
to sort ingredients for the pangs,
when came a bitter-sweet assault
and lured the fair maiden astray.

A tale of woe repeated in jest,
like salad served cold,
crispier lettuce, solid greens,
a soul market was heard afar.

Let laughter kiss your pain,
or hide it for shame,
as the family stole
its own harsh winters.

When Winter flew

When winter flew
past the burning logs of wood,
prancing through hearths and warm hands,
and daughters bid their friends a good night.

Normal and new, fallow and frail,
a past instil,
condemned afresh,
affirmed a new cycle of life;
a father forgetting the few silver pieces.

A child cajoled, pampered like ghosts,
tear drops, sparkling like jewellery;
small price to pay,
for a gun to carry.
You take this load

and these risks
and this gold
and these medals,
and I will shadow you forever.

When a Priest Invites You to Dinner

Secrets seldom have hope—
ask your friendly neighbourhood priest,
as they receive in remorse, both
hope and dawn in reverse.
Sun rays accentuating your piety,
as the men in cloaks,
singe indelible dark spots onto your palm.

Pity he stared at you, an
exodus revealed the epistles;
strange brown eyes, you thought,
a piercing inquest in plain sight.
You knew then,
he would invite you,
and serve you dinner in a casserole.

The Rain Prayer

When a bad harvest was just round the corner,
and yesterday's grains were left over,
no rodents could chew what man could swallow.
So the cats waved from the banyan tree,
above the granary, hanging
and humming, a contented purr,
as they await a feast below.

Darned soil and rain delayed,
a truant, messing with life, with food,
it was not so unkind, untimely
as the fertility of the land,
dependant on the harmonious water of life.

'Hurry up, you lazy frog,
live your lie or be gone,
put your slimy skin to rest!
Don't you need the rain more than us?'

This was the rain prayer,
recited by a widow in a farm,
down the wet banks
of river Doyang.

An Unnatural Outbreak

So then it came, as sure as night comes
Stealthily, it saw the indifferent herds,
no firstborns, but the young and the old;
in cold pastures lay the seed,
shredded, devoid, depleted of vitality.

Cursing like the ten plaques,
unleashed an ominous burden,
upon the doubting notions of capacity,
world-class science, smart tech,
on inexhaustible solutions,
and all the glory.

Like doomsday sightings,
locusts swarms the cities,
Nile turns red,
and as a retiree brushed his teeth,
in dim morning, Death claimed the first victim.

His firm teeth were not the cause
of a citizen's uproar,
the soft whimper, churning,
as the clamour reached new decibels,
and people cursed the science
and the prophet alike.

A retiree now, a loving widow,
a household, and an entire hospital;
swiftly it came and took them down,
creating space in the distance,
Meanwhile, learning as you suffer,
suffering as you wait
waiting as you experience death without dying.

Tests reports and testing times,
matching the doom and doomsayers
soars the bird of panic, so high.
In every corner a whispered disdain.

We looked on as it laid a timely wreath.

Inside All of It

Confusion ran deep within the hallowed halls
of purgatory.
Dimly lit, stretchers rattling the corridor,
white uniform—a hose, shiny black shoes,
suffocating cap,
all draped—and a weary body.
What a limbo to be in!

Oxygen,
short of air and breath,
unaware, life squeezed out of you.
clank, the chime of rusty bells;
they should be ringing.
Instead,
a struggle, like a sore,
in gasps, suffocating.

They took her away dead,
lifeless, limp, hapless, body,

Organ failure; their words lacking remorse,
sans a whimper of consolation,
pointing,
forefinger aimed at the caskets,
lined outside the hospital gate.

As though waiting,
waiting for long, anytime, a moment,
only striking a commotion, a confusion
in the hallowed halls.
Bandages rolling as it were,
where you seek a cure, a disaster befalls;
a purgatory on earth.

Private

Private spaces, public partners,
are of one stream; a virulent direction it takes,
seamless, sees no relation,
meets no realistic expectations.
Hosting a need,
breeding a cherished dream in absentia.
How much longer, how soon will people rest?
A bed only lasts as long as they need.

Simple gain and complicated loss,
worried man and worried institutions,
worried still the dependants,
and the children, and the pets,
and the entire ecosystem.

You take and you extract,
and you manage a flamboyance with grace.
On the pulpit of desolation, you shine,
but morals escaped your body too long ago.

And yet, your private margins need public fleecing,
your established norms seek further collection.
And when no enforcer is willing,
you take on that role too.

Such is your beauty, your eminence, your misfortune.

Grief is not yours—to give, to distribute
in the pale of doom
that awaits us on the visit we make.

Hope,
escorting the pig to slaughter,
or not;
and yet, with the doubts.

Healing was never found in your bosom,
in your advancement, in your instruments,
in your 'latest' toy of a pride.

Common Burden

Miracles?

Yes,
you feel them sometimes,
down the road
the calvary or oblivion.
Seems awkward and new,
but it could happen soon too.
And you pray for more
to come your way.

Distractions, enormous and proportionate,
obligations and obedience,
walk side by side.

You wish to carry
a charitable weight;
hence, awaiting you,
a sign is given, a sacrament—

And you, you cede to it anyway,
you accept without remorse.

It is no ordinary secret to hold
when petals wither away
from your palms,
a cascading flow,
and an unnecessary step,
fills the vacuum.
A crescent of nothingness.

You'd think miracles are special to people fading endlessly.

Assurance

Impervious Goliath,
never sought the aid
of the Ethiopians or the Egyptians,
haughty as the Philistines were
in the shadow of the imposing giant.
I'd rather think
of rose gardens in the deserts
or atop the Pyramids,
where few sadists belonging to a secret society plan a rebirth.

And should one doubt Goliath's significance,
one only has to go thus far
as Saul's wretchedness;
far worse than Macbeth it would seem,
such a modern warpath of petty affairs.

Queen

Queen Sheba;
will she be the Goliath reborn?
as much as God decreed David anointed,
generations feed from her bosom
even as Solomon passes away.
This bitter taste of a miracle.
For every Queen Sheba there was a Bethsheba.

The rustle of vanity;
virtue means less to the soul,
and in the tumult of it all, the jest of a tornado—
the Korean tornado—not of weather induced,
the beer poured over malt.
As you gulped it down
in one swig;
a bravado only the insane would indulge.

Queen Sheeba,
intoxicated,
yet the wine, herself, and her skin,
entraps the curious onlooker;
as Solomon saw it waste away.

Now, in Ethiopia,
the coffee arabica intoxicates,
in eternal gratitude.

In Waiting

Such bravados are but modern
such as Solomon and David would abhor.
Would they allow to be beguiled by seduction—
A slip, a miss, an error of judgement?

Is destiny and choice,
like diving deep into a pit, full of fire?
Another thought comes hither—
the obedience of David
is also his humble submission.
A bluest confession,
a bloody assumption,
Yet, all to the will of God.

It was for Goliath,
his first kill,
worst in store,
battlefields and victories,

thirst and honor,
obedience to such will,
opportunities missed by such choice.

Nevertheless, he will not smite the King anointed.

The Anointed

Such a fortunate man,
mortified by his own envy,
his brittle jealousy too;
blind man,
sees power in the earthly crown.

Harm the soul,
with sane intentions;
son butchered,
suicide taking him.
Saul, certainly, a tragedy of those times.

Shuttling between abyss and promise is
the pain of obedience;
negating patience is deceit.

Again, as the thunder rolls
And imaginations soar,
schizophrenic palpitations, hazy dreams, Patience resurfacing,

obedience a pain,
its loose strands tease you as
it dances to the erratic breeze.

Songs

When grandma sang,
a hymn, another chant,
a seed-sowing folk song,
a lullaby for me and the pup next door.
I would gladly sit,
elated, cushy on her thighs,
as only a grandson would.

Still as the dawn,
empty and eerie,
as I have seen little storms
take the peace out of my grandpa.

The sky rumbling, a dark thunder,
the night is louder, the snakes hissing higher,
the flashes incipient, the memories of sins—
almost kneeling, almost praying,
And the fragile heart, almost weeping.

Sleep and Prayer

The horses neigh, the cocks crow,
a freakish tormentor—
as if life were devoid of some.

A little creak—'Burmese teak, I must say'—
startles the priest,
praying,
sometimes out of habit.
This,
the folks down at the Baptist church used to say.

In unison, only the reverends
agree to see
a calmer sea
wresting control over the unruly thunder—
as if it never needed Noah.

In the sunny morning,
when rest reaches the pillow

softly beckoning you,
bury your nose, sink your head,
pray when you rise;
even for a minute longer,
savour the ache,
till you leap into your dreams.

Prayer, folks, it is prayer,
to laze afresh in the bosom of your pillows.

Acknowledgements

Special thanks to Nimrei, Athem and Yanmi for the never-ending coffee, food and patience during the writing of these poems. For the promptings and endless conversation on poetry, I thank Peter. For the time and love afforded me by Noying and Lumchi and Pao, I cannot be but grateful, since this would not have existed without them. And, finally to my editor Dibakar Ghosh, for all the wonderful suggestions, his efficiency, and for the warmth and friendship.

2